Rupert the DINOSAUR
the
on the Allotment!

This book belongs to

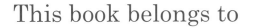

....

In an ancient forest
lives a little dinosaur
called Rupert.

He spends his days
eating vegetables and insects.

While at night
he sleeps
under
the
stars.

One morning, he notices that the forest is getting crowded with other creatures.

"*There are only so many our little world can feed,*" thinks Rupert.

So off he and his friends wander in search of food.

They stumble upon vast open fields full of Rupert's favourite food...vegetables.

He munches away, but his poor little friends, Dougie, Freddie and Birdie are not so lucky - there are no insects to be eaten at all.

Trudging from field to field, they come across something they have never seen before...

a city!

But still no sign of food.

Then, up ahead, from the sky...

3

...Birdie can see something wonderful:
an allotment!

Their very own dinosaur supermarket.

Off they sprint.

Getting closer, they creep into the allotment.

WHOOSH!

A pigeon
launches out
from the
cabbage patch.

The bushes rustle, the plants shake, and all manner
of bugs scurry and squirm, buzz and wriggle.

Now everyone has plenty to eat.

They eat and eat until their bellies are full,
under the stars they fall asleep.

Just like home from home.

In the morning, they are woken up by something
they have never heard before... human voices;

"Just thought to pop over
and lend a hand, Cashy."

"Thanks, Neville."

As the dinosaurs hide out of sight, a big black cloud moves across the sky.

"Look at that lovely rainbow."
Maddie points out to John and Ken.

The colours are just the same as Birdie's.

So from that day on,
Rupert calls Birdie
by a nickname:
Rainbow.

The storm cloud floats away.

But what's this now?

It's fast, low and noisy...

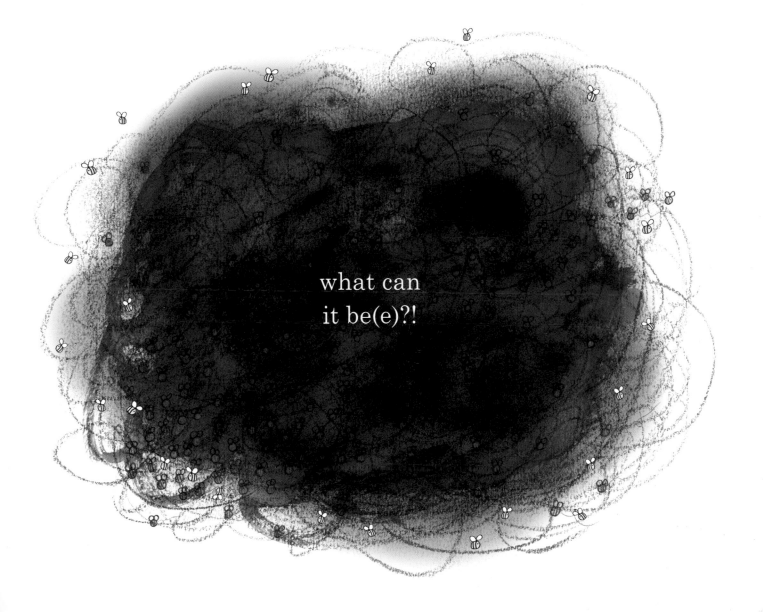

what can
it be(e)?!

A cloud of angry buzzing bees busily buzz by!!

Soon zipping out of sight.

Rupert, Dougie, Freddie and Rainbow
peep out of their hiding place.

Hurriedly, they snaffle up
all the insects they can find,
before curling up to sleep.

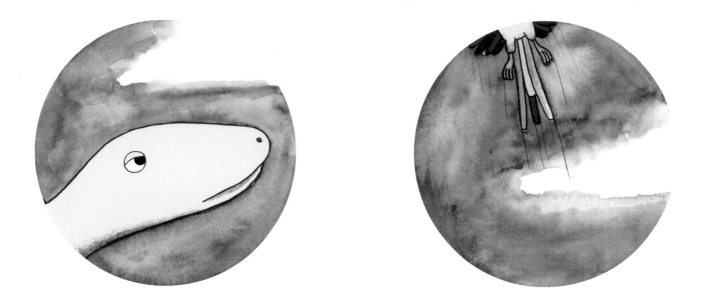

BANG! WALLOP! BANG!

Another noisy day shakes them awake.

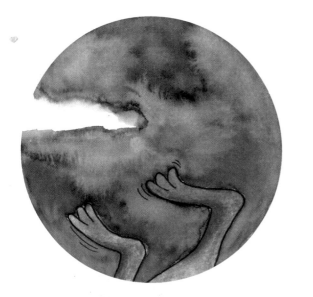

EMERGENCY MEETING
BEES HIVED OFF....
INSECTS LEGGED IT
NO MORE POLLINATION!!!

What will happen?

- Runner beans..............run out
- Shallots ....had their lot
- Cucumbers.................numbered
- We will be pressed for apples
- It's a dark day for blackberries
- We will have to shell out on peas
- And as for raspberries.............
                they'll be blown!!!

With all the insects gone,
Rupert's friends must find something else to eat.

Something everyone can share.

Something tasty.

Not crunchy, slimy, yucky
slugs and snails. .

Just then,
a beautiful
butterfly
flutters by...

...and lands on a flower.
Rainbow thinks to give it a try.

WOWILLISCIOUS!

So tasty, she doesn't even notice
her powder covered face, until...

AAA-TISHOOOO!!!

The pollen lands in the other flowers all around.

Grown ups call this pollination.

Dougie and Freddie try vegetables and fruit... *"Mmmmm, yummy, why didn't we ever eat these before?"* They think.

As all the plants begin to flower, the bees and bugs return to feed, pollinating as they eat. More and more vegetables and fruits grow...plenty for everyone.

Soon, autumn blows in
and winter approaches.

The insects find their winter hideaways, just like a lot
of animals that crawl into snuggly holes to sleep.

Grown ups call this
hibernating.

With less and less at the allotment to eat,
Rupert, Dougie, Freddie and Rainbow,
set off once again, in search of food...

...and shelter for the winter.

Just the place to take a well-earned rest
after this busy-buzzy adventure.

Rupert the Dinosaur

The first in the series.
An evolutionary tail,
with a long, curly, twist.

Read all about it at our website
www.rupertthedinosaur.com

Dedicated to:
My allotment friends: John, Ken, Cashy, Neville, Maddie, John, James, Sheridan, Nobby and Julia
(Doug Vallgren)

My green fingered Grandad, Maurice (Karl Newson)

First published in Great Britain in 2015
by Vallgren Publishing (Norwich)
12 The Avenues, Norwich, Norfolk, NR2 3PH
email dougvallgren@hotmail.co.uk
www.rupertthedinosaur.com

A CIP catalogue record of this book is available from the British Library upon request

ISBN 978-0-9927347-1-8 paperback

Printed and bound in Norwich by The Really Useful Print Company 01603 629796